NATALIE D'AMORE

Late Night Bites!

Prologue

1985

"You ready babe?" Frank asked, unlocking the front door. Amelia looked up at the fresh brick and mortar building, their own personal radio station. It had a neon sign that read *"The Lair".* Frank opened the door and motioned for Amelia to walk in with him, causing her to take a step back.

"What if we're terrible? Maybe this is a bad idea..Is it too late to cancel the lease?"

Frank smiled at her and grabbed her hand. "Don't worry about that. Just come in and look around, please?"

Amelia followed Frank inside and looked around the lobby. She saw a large red and gold bubble chandelier hanging from the ceiling, a variety of band posters hung on the walls, a white shag carpet and a couple of red leather chairs sat in the middle of the room.

"Frank, this is amazing."

Frank smiled and walked Amelia down the hall, showing the sound studio and then the office. On the desk was a bottle of champagne and two glasses. They celebrated their first night on air and for that year they were doing well. Top ratings non-stop and some high end sponsors came through. Sadly, as quickly the money came it was gone just the same.

Travis Duncan, Frank's friend, had knocked on the office door. "Hey, do you have a minute?" Frank looked at Travis and nodded, "Yeah, come in." Travis walked over to the desk and sat in one of the chairs, placing a clipboard in front of Frank. "These are these months' ratings and they are rough, and I'm being gentle with that." Frank took the clipboard and looked. All he saw was red, bad feedback comments and low viewings.

"Shit," Frank groaned. "Has Amelia seen this yet?"

Travis shook his head.

"What am I going to do?"

~knock knock~

Frank and Travis looked at the door and saw a man wearing a black suit. The man stood at 6' with dark Red hair, a face filled with a beard and mustache, and a pair of red rounded sunglasses covered his eyes.

"I hope you don't mind, the front door was unlocked and I let myself in." Frank and Travis looked at each other.

"Who are you," Frank asked, standing up from his chair.

The man smiled and took his glasses off. "I go by many names, you may call me Mason." Mason opened his jacket and placed the glasses in his pocket. "I heard through the grapevine that you are having some trouble with your station."

Frank looked at Travis in confusion. "Um well yeah, we just got our ratings for the past month and they are rough."

Mason nodded in agreement,"So I've heard, but I can help with that if you'd like." Travis stood up and cautiously approached Mason. "How so?"

Mason smiled, his Bourbon colored eyes flickered with delight. "Oh nothing crazy, I'll meet with some sponsors of mine and we will help you for a very *small* price."

Frank raised an eyebrow. "What's the price?"

Mason shrugged, "Nothing big, just some favors that you'll have to do but like I said nothing crazy."

To Melody Toppins, thank you for showing Dr. Ros & Mrs. Wilson my 'Frankenstein' paper in High School. To my husband Ray, for just listening to my madness. Angela Yukiro Smith, for reading through all my word vomit chapters and working with me. To my mom and dad, for always dealing with my crazy writing ideas and still loving me. And to my son, I love you to the moon and back.

Frank and Travis looked at each other. "Should we do it?" Travis asked. Frank looked at the picture of him and Amelia and then Mason.

"Do you have the con-" before Frank could finish, Mason had pulled out a contract and handed it to him. Frank noticed a tattoo that resembled a canine skull in the middle of a cross on the back of his hand. Frank and Travis looked at the contract, signed it and handed it to Mason. Mason smiled ear to ear, showing his sharp canines.

He took his sunglasses out of his pocket, put them on and left the office.

"See you around kiddies."

Chapter 1

_2022_

Michelle looked into her bathroom mirror as she was getting ready for work. She had a love/hate relationship with being a late night host: with her being a night owl she could stay up all night to play and talk about her favorite music while getting paid: crappy pay but enough to keep the lights on and food in the kitchen, she doesn't have to worry about looking professional.

She could show up in her pajamas and no one would bat an eye. Barely any callers and the ones that do call in are just looking for the adult hotline. She pinned her hair up and fixed her make-up. She heard her phone ringing and checked the caller ID. _Boss Man._ She groaned and rolled her eyes. "Hey Frank," she answered.

"Hey Mich," he said," are you still comin' in tonight?" Michelle could hear him rummaging through papers on the other side of the phone.

"Yes, or at least I'm supposed to because that's what the plan was for the last show."

Frank coughed over the phone. "Ok, because I'm not going to be able to make it in… but I've got a guy comin' in to help you set up and stuff." He coughed again so hard Michelle could practically feel it through the phone. She grimaced at the sound of his coughing. The sound of him coughing reminded her of her grandfather whenever he would cough and spit would land on her face. She shuddered at the reminder.

"Ok, well I'm about to head down there so I guess I'll see the new guy when I get there." No response from Frank, just the sound of him hanging up. Michelle rolled her eyes and finished getting ready.

Michelle grabbed her bag and keys and headed out the door. As she headed down the stairs, one of her neighbors noticed her coming down as he was making his way up the stairs and fixed his hair. They both caught each other's attention and greeted one another with a casual smile and nod.

"Hey Michelle," he greeted softly, "You heading out?"

Michelle and Derek had been neighbors in the same building for the past couple of years. He helped her move in and was the first one to welcome her to the building. When COVID happened, he helped her with groceries and getting around town when she needed to.

"Hey Derek and yes. Another night shift beckons me."

Derek adjusted his computer bag on his shoulder. "Oh cool. I'll have to tune in for tonight's show then."

Michelle always knew that Derek had a soft spot for her. She was flattered by how he treated her. "Yeah but we got a new guy coming in the studio tonight, so I'm not sure how things are going to go."

"We'll if it's your night on, then it'll be a good show, like always," Derek assured. Michelle smiled and continued walking down the stairs. As she approached the front door, she felt a cold wind on the back of her neck. Thinking a bug had crawled on her, she reached back to grab it but she felt nothing. She turned around thinking that someone was grabbing for her but saw no one. She looked up the stairs and only saw Derek, still at his door fighting for it to unlock so he could go in.

"I'll see you in the morning, don't stay up late if the show sucks." Derek chuckled as his door finally opened and he walked inside his apartment. Michelle left her apartment building and started walking down to the radio station.

When Michelle got to the building and walked in, she could hear a distorted version of *Mr.Crowley* by Ozzy Osbourne playing over the intercom. She looked at the overhead speakers confused. The speakers had been busted since COVID and no one wanted to pay to get them fixed. She walked upstairs to the studio and saw a man standing in the hallway.

"Who the hell are you?"

The man looked at her and held his hands up. "Whoa!! Hold on!! I'm Nick. Frank called me in to help you run the studio tonight."

"You're the new guy?"

Nick stood at about 5'9", slim build and looked like he weighed in at 80 lbs wet. He had dark reddish auburn hair. "Yep I'm from a station downtown. I listen to your guys' station a lot," he said, taking his jacket off and placing it on the hook in the office. "Our station is more of a new age self help type station."

"I see," Michelle said, "Well, I'm Michelle, but when I'm on air I go by Skully Riot."

Nick shook her hand but his eyes grew wide and his jaw dropped at the mention of Skully Riot. He looked at her, processing the information. He not only thought he would ever meet the famous night mother known as Skully Riot, but that she also looked like she listens to POP music and camps outside for pumpkin spice lattes and Taylor Swift concert tickets.

"Wait..YOU are Skully Riot?"

Michelle nodded. "Yep, the one and only." She placed her bag in a chair and took her jacket off, "Sorry to disappoint a fan."

Nick shook his head. "No, far from disappointed! Just surprised. When you hear Skully Riot, you think of an Elvira-with-a-mohawk type of character, but you are very much the opposite."

Michelle looked at her outfit: a worn and torn Metallica t-shirt, black denim jeans and dark brown boots. She looked in her compact mirror and fixed her messy chestnut brown hair. "I didn't think I looked that bad through the radio." Nick smirked and rolled his eyes.

"So what's the plan for tonight's schedule?" he asked, grabbing a notepad. "Since Frank is out, you are the boss and your word is law." Michelle smiled at his devotion.

"You know if I open my own radio studio, I think I might keep around. Just a warning though, I can be a bit of a bitch to work with especially if I don't have an IV bag full of coffee on standby by the time I clock on."

Nick pretended to take notes in his notebook, "Note to self: keep the coffee IV on drip and standby".

Michelle chuckled as she pulled out her notebook from her bag and looked over the schedule and playlist for the final show.

Michelle went over her notes. "Well to be honest with you, tonight is actually our last night on the air," she said as they walked down to the broadcasting studio. "The plan is to play some good music, get crappy take out in between breaks and talk about some good memories with the studio."

Nick looked at Michelle confused,"Wait, tonight's your last night?"

Michelle nodded, "Yep. We thought when COVID hit we'd

still be in business because we'd be able to do everything at home, but then everybody started jumping on the podcast and recording industry train and our studio fell in the dust. So like I said, we're gonna play some good music, tell some good stories, eat some crappy take out and do it all on the clock."

She smiled as she sat in her leather studio chair, noticing all the wear and tear in the crevices. Her heart felt heavy, remembering that this is where she started and this is where it was going to end. She remembered staying up in middle school and high school to listen to the late night stories they would tell over the radio. She looked at all the posters of her as Skully Riot.

"I am going to miss this though," she said with a half smile. She turned on the station, the lights flickered and buzzed on. She made her adjustments to the music board and her microphone. She looked at Nick and nodded to him, "You ready?"

"Let's fuck this chicken," he joked.

She busted out laughing and took a breath to calm herself. She looked at the "On Air" sign and flipped another switch, making the red light come on. She took one more breath and smiled.

"Hello there, my little late night parasites. It's your night mother like no other, Skully Riot. In case you missed our voicemails, tonight is our last night on air. I know my little pretties, it broke my heart when I got the call too. So tonight, we're gonna have some fun on the clock. We're going to play some of our favorite hits and tell some funny stories about the behind the scenes of the studio. We're goin' to start the night off with something simple and one of my personal favorites, *Maneater* by Hall & Oates. I know it's a shocking revelation, but I wasn't always a rock addict… but we'll get to that later. So sit back and relax and we'll dig you back up when it's over."

Chapter 2

Lexi Powers sat at the tall bar, watching and admiring her reflection in the mirror behind the bartender. The bartender noticed and smirked.

"I see you're on the hunt again Lex," he joked, "Be careful. It's a full moon and all the crazies are out."

Lexi rolled her eyes at Mic. Even though they had been friends since High School, give or take a decade, they always looked out for each other. Lexi played with her empty glass as Mic worked on making her a new one.

"I'm working on it. Just make sure you at least find a cute one to steal from tonight, I hate when they ugly cry."

Lexi giggled as she looked around the bar. She noticed the usual patrons but no one stuck out to her.

"Nothing but duds as far as I can see".

Mic placed a hand on hers and patted it. "It's okay, one day you will find that special toad and hopefully not give you warts." He teased as she smacked his hand away.

"Screw you Mic," Lexi chuckled as Mic went back to making drinks. She scrunched her freshly bleached platinum hair up and pulled down the deep plunged dress that showed more skin than a bathing suit.

"Look, all I'm saying is there's always a bunch of jerks out here looking for women like you to get a hold of and take them away. I love you like a sister, I just want you safe." Mic turned on the radio and *Maneater* was playing.

Lexi scoffed and rolled her eyes. "Jesus, I can't believe they had Michelle host the last show tonight. I should've been hosting tonight."

Mic looked over at her confused. "Then why aren't you?"

Lexi looked at her drink and shrunk a little in her seat. "Let's just say Amelia got pissed because Frank asked for some special "favors" and I did them." Lexi wiped her tears and fixed herself up again.

She glanced around the bar and started her hunt. A couple of men caught her eye, but she could tell they had already drunk their money away. She had been doing this for most of her adult life, and she could tell whose pockets were full for grabbing and whose weren't worth the moths that came out of them. She glanced at her watch and noticed it was almost 9 o'clock. She got up and walked to the bathroom, closed the door behind her and looked in the mirror. She fixed her lipstick and applied some pheromone perfume to her neck and ear lobe.

She was walking back to her seat when a man stumbled into her, almost knocking her over. She could practically smell the booze coming from his pores.

"I'm sorry," he mumbled.

Her heart fluttered when she noticed the gold chain around his neck. She helped the man stand up straight, catching a glimpse of his face. Although he towered over her, she could see his sun kissed skin and his eyes were a light Hazel green color. His shaggy hair was brown with little specks of white throughout his hair. He also had some stubble growing in some spots, at least a few days old and way past a 5 o'clock shadow.

"Are you okay," she asked in a semi concerned tone.

The man mumbled and cursed under his breath. He fixed his shirt and jacket and looked at Lexi. Her crystal blue eyes beamed up at him, almost as if they were hypnotizing him to look at nothing else but her and her alone. He had to stop himself from looking lower to what was supposed to be her dress but was barely passing off as a couple of napkins.

He nodded. "Yeah, I'm alright," he groaned. He stumbled to the ground. She gasped and helped him back up. She helped him up by his arm and started walking him back to the bar she was sitting at.

"You must be having a fun night," she joked.

The man looked at her confused. "Yeah you can say that," he said as she walked him over to her seat. Mic watched as the two sat down.

Mic looked at Lexi with a raised eyebrow. "Good evening, you two. What can I get you?"

Lexi smiled at the man. "What you drinkin' sugar?"

The man looked at Lexi then at Mic and shrugged. "Um... scotch is fine."

Lexi winked at Mic. "And you already know what I like." Mic rolled his eyes and went off to make their drinks.

Lexi held out her hand to the man. "I'm Lexi," she beamed. The man looked at her hand then at her eyes, which had an eager and pleading look to them. He could tell something was up but wasn't entirely sure what her intentions were. He was beginning to think she was one of those women that lures men back to her place, drugs them and the next thing he knows he's waking up in a tub of ice missing a body part. But he knew he could take her in a fight if need be.

"I'm Jack," he said, shaking her hand. Jack looked at Lexi,

confused as to why such a woman was giving him so much attention. She kept her bright smile on as she adjusted in her seat. Jack watched her as she squirmed trying to get situated on the barstool. Her movements caused her breasts to bounce and peak out of the fabric.

"So Jack, are you hungry?" Lexi asked. Jack raised an eyebrow, uncomfortable.

"Look Lexi, you're sweet for getting me a drink but I'm not looking to hire a woman for the night."

Lexi looked at Jack, acting offended. "You think I'm a hooker." That question made Jack sober quickly.

"Oh my god, I'm so sorry I didn't mean to offend you. I'm not used to women making the first move."

Lexi smiled softly. "It's alright Jackie. Have some dinner with me and we'll call it even." Jack smiled awkwardly and nodded. Mic walked back over to Lexi and Jack and placed the drinks in front of them.

"Would you guys like some food too?" he asked. Lexi smiled, "We'll take a couple of burgers, maybe some nachos too." Mic walked away again and placed the order.

Jack looked at Lexi impressed. "You like to take charge, don't you?" Lexi shrugged. "Sometimes. If I don't, then who will?"

Jack nodded and sipped on the fresh whiskey. The food came a few moments later and they started their meal. "You know Lexi, I have to say I've enjoyed your company and I apologize if I've been curt with you," Jack said wiping his mouth, "It's just you reminded me of my wife and it just stirred up some memories." Lexi had taken a bite out of a fry and swallowed quickly. "Your wife? Are you still together or divorced?"

Jack shook his head solemnly. "No, she actually passed away three years ago tonight," he said while playing with his food,

"This is actually where we had our first date and I just wanted some good memories here." Jack hung his head low and wiped his eyes, "I'm sorry, I don't mean to trauma dump on you after only knowing you for five minutes."

Lexi smiled softly and gave him a quick hug. "It's ok, don't be sorry for mourning. You should be able to heal how you wanna heal." She patted his back and they finished dinner. Mic dropped the tab between them but gave Lexi a glance telling her that she better not pull her bullshit tricks with this one. Jack reached for his wallet but Lexi grabbed his hand.

"No don't you dare, I offered you dinner. I will pay for you," she insisted while handing a card and the bill to Mic. Jack smiled. "Thank you Lexi, that's very kind of you," he said adjusting in his seat,"would it be ok if I walked you home?" Lexi smiled and nodded. "Absolutely, let me just go powder my nose and then we'll head out."

Lexi got up from her seat and made her way to the bathroom. Mic dropped the card and receipt in front of Jack. "Oh this is actually her card, I'll wait for her to come back," Jack said. Mic looked at him confused, "Your name is Jack right?" Jack raised an eyebrow and nodded. "Yeah..why?" Mic looked at the card and pointed to the name on it: Jack Smythe.

"What the fuck," he cursed under his breath. He pulled out his pockets and saw that his wallet was on the ground behind him. He opened it and saw all his cash and other cards were gone. *Son of a bitch.* Jack looked at the bar and saw that Lexi had forgotten something on her way out.

Lexi made her way down the road, counting her newly claimed cash and smiling with delight. She rolled up the cash and placed it in her coat pocket. She hummed as she turned down the alley to her apartment building. She reached inside her purse for keys, only to discover they weren't there. She checked inside her coat pockets for them. She knew she had them when she left the bar because she could hear and feel them bounce inside the purse as she walked. She looked around thinking they might have fallen out around the stairs but still saw no sign of them anywhere. She grabbed her phone but realized her phone had died at some point during the night. "Shit." She said, stomping her foot.

She rummaged through her purse with frustration, before emptying it onto the sidewalk. She got on her knees and searched the scattered contents. Lipstick: Check. Wallet: Check. Phone: Check. No keys were to be seen.

~JINGLE JINGLE~

Lexi's heart stopped. In front of her were a pair of steel toed boots. She looked up to see Jack's stone sober face.

"Missing these?" he asked in a menacing tone. He dropped them on the ground in front of her and as she reached for them, he placed a foot on them and kicked them away into the darkness.

"Whoops."

She flinched and her body tensed up, her heart felt cold and her stomach was in knots. She started to shake she as she felt one of his hands touch the top of her head, gently stroking her hair. Of all the times she's done this, a man never followed her or even tried to find her. Her chest felt tight and her heart started to pound, she wasn't sure if it was her going into fight or flight mode or if she was about to actually die on her front door step and no one would know.

"Jack," she whimpered, "I'm sorry. I still have all of your cash. Please take it back. I'm sorry."

Jack tilted his head. "You know, right now you remind me

even more of my wife. She begged like this too."

The hairs on Lexi's arms and the back of her neck stood straight up when those words left his mouth. She looked into Jack's eyes and noticed they were all black. He grinned, showing his teeth shift into sharp daggers.

"Jack."

He grabbed her by the hair and dragged her into the darkness. She screamed and kicked as hard as she could. She swung her fist through the air, hoping to land at least one hit to try to break away. She felt his hand wrap around her neck, taking the breath away from her and something sharp and burning pierced into her neck.

~Crunch, Squelchhhhh~

She screamed in pain and went limp. Her body fell against the hard concrete and she started to feel cold. She watched as Jack got up and walked into the light, wiping her blood off his face. His eyes went back to their normal hazel green color and he smirked as she lay there. Her vision started to blur and darken as she watched him walk back to the main part of the alley, whistling *Maneater* as he turned the corner and disappeared.

Chapter 3

Nick gave Michelle the thumbs up and flipped the "On Air" switch, turning the red light on once more. "And we're back. In case you decided to get off your ass and turn on the radio, tonight's our last night on the air so we're going to make it worth our while."

Michelle said grabbing her notebook and flipping through her pages of notes, "Now we're going to start the history portion of tonight's segment. Don't worry there's no pop quiz so everybody passes."

"Our lovely crypt of a studio, *The Lair*, opened its doors back in 1985 by our fearless leaders Frank and Amelia Nettles. Frank handled the paperwork while Amelia lent out her voice for the first decade running. Then Lexi Powers picked up the torch in 1996, Vince Rails in 2006 and he continued all the way till 2016 when your girl finally got her chance to pick up the mic."

Michelle looked at the pictures on the wall of all the hosts and remembered all the fun memories of everyone being together before COVID and her heart sank a little.

"I've only been with the studio since 2016 but I can tell you guys that these ghouls became such a big part of my family and taught me everything I know. I wouldn't be where I am without them, so as a way to say thank you I wanna dedicate this next song. Frank and Amelia, wherever you two are, thank you for starting this station and bringing us awesome music." Michelle reached next to her and pressed the play button and *Who made Who* by ACDC started playing.

***

Frank and Amelia sat in their living room, Frank in his leather recliner and Amelia in her flowery loveseat. Amelia looked at the clock that hung over the bookcase. The last show had just started.

"Frank, do you want me to turn on the radio?" she asked, "For old times sake?"

Frank grimaced and shook his head. "No just let them do the show," he grumbled as he changed the channels. Amelia sat back in her seat and went back to reading her book.

~knock knock~

Frank and Amelia looked at the door then at each other. "Who the hell is that," he complained, getting out of his recliner and waddling over to the door. He opened the door and saw a young woman with jet black hair, red lips and sun kissed skin standing there. "What do you want?"

The woman smiled.

"Good evening, my name is Lamia. I believe we have some business to discuss." She pulled a card from her pocket and handed it to Frank. He snatched it out of her hand and took one look at it: it was a symbol that had a canine skull and a cross behind it.

Frank's heart stopped as he crumbled the card up and threw it at the woman. "GET THE HELL OUT OF HERE!!!!" He slammed the door and locked it then ran to the back door, making sure it was locked and closed the curtains.

Amelia watched Frank in confusion and fear as to why he was doing all of this. "Frank, what is going on?" Frank didn't respond, just kept checking the locks and then he grabbed a gun from the bookcase.

He checked the revolver and counted the bullets. Frank pulled Amelia up from her seat and pushed her towards the hallway. "Amelia go hide," he pleaded. Amelia looked at Frank. "Frank what the hell is going on," she asked frantically.

~BANG! BANG!~

Amelia screamed and Frank pulled her to the bedroom and shoved her in. "Lock this door and do not come out,"he ordered, "No matter what." He pulled the door closed and ran back to the living room.

~BANG! BANG! BANG!~

The final bang sent the door flying off the hinges and across the living room. Frank ducked behind the couch and hid. He could hear Lamia's heels click against the stone floor then become muffled when she walked onto the carpet.

"Frankie dear,' she called out, "You know the boss does not like these types of games." Amelia poked her head from the bedroom door and saw Lamia looking around the living room for Frank. She made her way to the couch where Frank was hiding and grinned at him as he looked up at her.

"Hiya Frankie."

Lamia grabbed Frank by his shirt collar and dragged him to the middle of the room. He layed sprawled on his back, groaning in pain.

Amelia walked closer to the living room, watching Lamia stand over Frank. "Frank, you made a deal. You haven't paid up so now I have to collect." She reached into her pocket, grabbed a cigarette out of a golden cigarette holder and lit one. She took a puff and exhaled.

"Now, you're lucky I'm feeling generous tonight so you can either come in peace OR we can just take care of business right here on the white carpet...your call." Frank looked at Lamia but heard a floorboard creak behind him. He looked back and saw Amelia behind him.

"Frank, what is she talking about?"

Lamia looked at Frank then at Amelia. "Oh Frankie never told you? He made a deal when you two opened the radio station," she took another puff of her cigarette and smiled. "Silly boy didn't read the fine print when it stated that if things went tits up, we come and collect."

Amelia looked at Frank. "But *I* never signed anything."

Lamia nodded, finished her cigarette and put it out on the carpet, leaving a small burnt circle. "True, however you were complicit in the deal when you brought those girls to his office after hours for, what did you call them... 'auditions'?" Amelia dropped to the ground on her knees when she heard those words.

Lamia shrugged nonchalantly. "Shame we have to do this the hard way because this is a very nice white carpet." She got up and walked over to the front door archway and stepped outside. She whistled into the night and an emaciated, decaying wolfhound walked through and sat by Frank and Amelia. The smell of burning and rotting flesh filled the room, causing them to gag and be sick. The dog looked at Lamia, awaiting orders.

She looked at the dog and smiled, "Who's a good boy? Are ya' hungry? Are you?"

The dog's skeletal bone tail started to wag, almost hitting

Amelia in the face but striking Frank on his chest, causing him to start bleeding. He screamed and the dog latched on to him. Amelia wailed and covered her eyes. The sounds of her husband's screams and flesh tearing caused her to hyperventilate and lay on the ground. Her husband went silent but she could feel the dog close to her face. The dog sniffed at her and nudged her with its blood drenched nose. Amelia whimpered and shook as she uncovered her eyes, staring at the dog's face.

The dog lunged at Amelia before she could do anything. Lamia waited for the dog to finish before whistling for him and walking outside to the black car that they came from. Jack waited for her and opened the rear door. She nodded in with a silent thank you and got in.

Chapter 4

"Hey Michelle, we've got a problem."

Michelle walked over to Nick and examined the sound booth. She checked everything and tested the sound and mics, no sound or audio was coming through. "How long has it been like this?"

"I noticed it about five minutes ago. I tried to troubleshoot everything but nothing seemed to be working." Nick tried flipping a fuse and turning the system on and off.

"Shit." Michelle took out her cell phone and tried to call Frank, only to be sent to voicemail. She inserted a tape into the system and it started playing *My Girl* by Nirvana.

"Dammit. Let me try Travis, our tech guy. If he can come in, great! Worst case scenario we switch to the prerecorded stuff and just finish the shift that way." She waited for a response from Frank or Travis but nothing was coming through.

* * *

"Where the hell were you?!?!" Delia flinched as Travis swiped all her stuff off her dresser, sending her jewelry flying across the room and causing her vanity mirror to shatter.

Travis paced back and forth, glaring at Delia and waiting for her response. She stayed silent. She knew that no matter what her answer was, right or wrong, she would be ending up on the floor with another bruise and a definite trip to the emergency room. The longer Travis didn't get a response, the more his rage boiled inside him. He snatched her phone away and stormed outside, slamming the door behind him.

She sobbed and buried her face in her hands. She could still hear him yelling outside at someone on her phone, then a shattering sound and him screaming. Static came over the radio and it started playing *My Girl*. Delia walked over to the radio.

She didn't remember turning it on earlier. She listened to the song and a sense of warmth came over her. She felt like she was standing in the sunlight after being stuck in a decade of winters. She felt her body go numb, and went into autopilot. Travis came back inside, huffing and puffing heavily.

"You happy now? I busted that damn phone because you wanted to talk to some ass named Richard." Travis saw Delia standing in front of the radio, frozen in place.

He walked over to her and grabbed her by the shoulder. She looked at him, her once brown eyes were now a smokey gray color, void of any life or emotion. "Delia?"

She just stared at Travis. He raised his hand to slap her out of it but she got the first hit. He staggered back and landed against the wall grabbing his nose, his hand was covered in blood and he could start to taste it in his mouth. He spit some blood out, along with a part of his tooth.

"What the fu-?!?!" He was cut off by a punch to the throat. He went down to his knees gasping for air as Delia turned the volume up on the radio. She walked over to the back door where they had a heavy antique iron as a doorstop and picked it up before walking back to Travis.

Travis watched Delia as she got closer to him. Her once nurturing but timid self was now ready to fight back and waited for him to get back up. Travis tried to pull himself up but she kicked him back to the ground. "Delia please. I'm sorry, for everything."

Her head tilted and she mocked his sobbing plea. She knelt down to him, barely brushing against his face. "I'm sorry I let you do this for so long."

Travis screamed as Delia raised the iron back and brought it down on him.

Thwack!

Travis fell prostrate. Delia raised the iron again and struck him harder, the louder Kurt sang the harder the hit. Travis' body finally collapsed, succumbing to his injuries as the song ended with a "Thank you" and the radio turned off. In his jacket pocket, his phone rang again.

Delia pulled the phone out of his pocket and pressed the ignore button before smashing it against the kitchen tile.

* * *

Michelle groaned as she checked her phone. "I'm still not getting anything from Travis. Do you want to go ahead and get our food while I switch everything over to the pre-recorded set?"

Nick agreed, took the order notes, and went out the door. Michelle switched the show, and with nothing else to do, decided that now was the time to walk around the station.

She never really had the opportunity to fully explore the radio station, but now was the perfect time. She made a lap around the halls, looking at the old band posters, staff pictures and concert tours they promoted over the years.

She finally made her way back to the office and walked in. There were a bunch of papers scattered everywhere, most of them were too faded to read. She opened a cabinet and saw an old Polaroid camera. It looked familiar but she never remembered anyone using it since she had started working on the station.

In another cabinet she found an old lock box. A cold chill crawled up her spine and the hairs stood up on the back of her neck. Her phone rang and she gave a quick shriek in surprise. Embarrassed, she cursed under her breath as checked the caller ID: Mic.

"Hey Mic, what's up?"

"Hey... did you hear about Lexi?"

Michelle was confused. She hadn't heard anything from anyone that night. "No, I've been at the station tonight and we don't have a TV or anything. Why? What happened?"

Mic sniffled and blew his nose. "She got attacked on the way home. She's dead."

Chapter 5

Michelle's heart and stomach dropped when she heard those words come through the phone. She collapsed in the old office chair, causing dust to puff into the air. "What do you mean she died?"

Mic sniffled and blew his nose again. "She came in tonight and scammed another guy. He was pissed and asked where she lived. I told him I didn't know. He ended up leaving a few minutes later." Mic blew his nose again and kept talking to one of his coworkers.

"One of her neighbors found her in the alley. The cops looked at security footage and saw some dog drag her there and attack her."

Michelle was silent for a moment, attempting to process the news. "Oh my god… have you told Frank and Amelia?"

Michelle didn't know Lexi well. By the time Michelle became a host, Lexi was already long gone from the studio. She remembered a time Lexi and Amelia had gotten into a fight, never heard the details, but saw them screaming at each other when she had walked in for her intern gig. Sometimes everyone would meet and hang out at the radio's favorite bar after hours but other than that Michelle hardly knew Lexi, only by reputation.

"No. I tried calling them but there was no answer."

Michelle sighed. "Ok I'll try calling them in a minute. If nothing else, I'll probably step out and go over there since we're down. I can let them know what happened."

Michelle and Mic said their goodbyes and hung up. Michelle checked on the radio and made sure they were still on the prerecorded tape.

She called Frank and Amelia but only heard a busy tone on the other end. She sighed and decided to try again later. She went back to the office to snoop around to see if she could find keys for the lockbox. She heard something crash behind her and she noticed a shelf had fallen off the wall and there was something on the floor shining in the office light: a pair of keys.

She picked them up and examined them, they seemed small enough to fit the lockbox. *Yeah this isn't how bad horror movies start.* She inserted the keys and the lockbox popped open with ease. *Well shit.*

She opened the box and saw bank notices, old thank you notes, and several Polaroid pictures of the hosts and special guests with Frank and Amelia. Some of them were too damaged to identify everyone.

She narrowed her eyes in an attempt to at least see some type of detail. She made out one picture of Frank and Amelia at one of their after shows wearing some masks and laughing. There were Halloween decorations and other people wearing masks. One person was completely naked and covered in fake blood, at least that's what Michelle was hoping it was.

She found a business card that had some weird logo on it: A cross with a canine skull. She flipped it around to find out what company this was but there was no name or information on it. She pulled out her phone, took a picture of the card and ran it through a search. Still nothing.

The overhead speaker screeched loudly to the point Michelle had to cover her ears. *You don't own me* by Leslie Gore started playing through the static then the sound of a door slamming shut echoed through the station. Michelle darted for the front door and shoved it open, almost running into Nick.

"Whoa, are you okay? What happened?"

Michelle leaned over to catch her breath, pointing inside and gasping for air. She reached in her back pocket and pulled out her inhaler. She took a puff, held it and exhaled, then repeated. "There's something inside there." As soon as she said that, there was a roaring sound and the front door slammed shut.

Nick dropped the food and stared at the door. "What the fuck?"

He tugged on the door and it wouldn't budge. He tried one more time but had gotten the same result. "What do we do?"

Michelle shrugged. "No idea but I think this is our cue to get the hell out of dodge." Nick agreed but they both quickly realized their stuff was still in the office. The door's lock clicked and it slowly opened. Nick and Michelle looked at each other.

"Snatch and grab?"

"Is there any other way?"

They both ran inside to the office, grabbed their stuff and ran back out the door. "We need to go talk to Frank and Amelia. I've been trying to call them all night since we've been having issues and I haven't heard anything back from either one of them."

Nick nodded in agreement and looked around for Michelle's car. "Where did you park?"

"I walked here... I might be a popular night host, but I'm not that popular."

Nick chuckled and signaled Michelle to follow him. They walked past a few cars and then reached a motorcycle. Michelle glanced at Nick. "You have a dirtbike? I pinned you more of Jeep or maybe a Prius type of guy."

Nick gave Michelle a fake gasp and insulted look. "Correction ma'am, this is a Honda 250 Bobber. I just got the engine rebuilt, the body repainted and she purrs like a kitten." Nick gave his bike an adoring tap, "It's ok baby, forgive her for she does not know the error of her ways."

Nick put his leather jacket and helmet on Michelle. "You don't have an extra one?" Nick shook his head, "Nah I'll be fine. I've been riding since I was 15." Nick climbed on and Michelle followed suit.

Nick turned the key and kick started the pedal. "By the way, how good is your health insurance?" Before Michelle could acknowledge the question, they were already off down the road.

Chapter 6

Michelle and Nick arrived at Frank and Amelia's house. As they got closer to the house, they found the front door was completely off its hinges and the house looked as if it was ransacked.

"Wait here," Nick said, pushing her back. Michelle ignored his order, pushed past him and walked straight in. The smell of copper hit Michelle and Nick's nose. They covered their noses with the collars of their shirts and walked further into the house.

Michelle made her way to the living room and stopped dead in her tracks, almost falling backwards when she saw the carnage in the middle of the room. The once pristine white carpet was now a dark crimson, matted crater of snarl. Frank and Amelia were barely recognizable, the only way she could tell who was who was by Amelia's manicure and Frank's jeans.

She ran back outside and to the bushes to vomit while Nick pulled his phone out and called 911. She wiped her mouth and spit the last of the vomit out. She looked down to make sure none got on her and she saw a crumpled piece of paper on the ground. She examined it and saw the logo with the cross and canine skull on it.

"Hey, the police are on the way. You ok?"

Michelle pulled the other card from her pocket and looked at both logos, everything matched. "No, not really. I think something bad happened here."

Nick looked from Michelle to the carnage in the house. "Well, the fact that there are two dead bodies behind us I don't think I can argue with you in that department."

Michelle rolled her eyes. "No shit. I'm talking about these." She gave Nick the two cards.

"Where did you find these?"

"One was from the station and the other was by the bushes."

Nick looked at them front to back. "Frank and Amelia never mentioned this company to you?"

Michelle shook her head. "Nope, and I know it's not a band logo either. Something is definitely going on."

The police showed up, followed by the coroner. They cleared the scene and took Nick and Michelle's statements.

"Do you know if anyone would want to hurt Frank or Amelia? Any enemies that they might have?"

Michelle thought for a moment. "Not that I know of. They weren't perfect people but they didn't deserve to die. However, I did find these business cards. One is from the station and the other one was by the bushes. I also found some pictures in my boss's office. I don't have them with me but they looked sketchy."

The detective placed the business cards in an evidence bag and handed them to an officer. "Thank you for your time. If you think of anything else or if you can bring those pictures to us, please reach out to us or come down to the station. The officer handed Nick and Michelle a card and went their separate ways.

Michelle stood there, dissatisfied and feeling ignored as she watched the detectives walk away. "Wait, that's it? You're done here?"

The detectives looked at each other then at Michelle. "Yes ma'am, for now. The other officers are taking some more statements and gathering evidence. The coroner is examining the scene and then he's taking the bodies to the morgue."

The detectives walked back to their car while the other officers finished taking statements, checking the scene and leaving right after. Nick and Michelle made their way back to the bike. Michelle hesitated before she climbed on to the bike.

She felt something cold touch her neck and she looked behind her. Nick noticed her reaction to something but couldn't tell what she was looking at. "You okay?"

She looked back at the house and watched a couple of straggling neighbors talking to a police officer on guard. "No I'm not. Two people were murdered and the police are acting like nothing happened."

Nick shrugged. "Well sometimes it's like that. Plus this type of stuff takes time for it to be investigated."

"But the officers that took our statements acted like they didn't care."

"Well they have been doing this a lot longer than us. This probably isn't their first murder mystery. We've done what we can for now. Let's just try to go back to the station and shut everything down."

Michelle walked back to the house and approached the officer. "Excuse me sir, but I was the one that called about this and I just realized that I had dropped my bag in there. Could I run in and grab it?"

The officer looked back and shook his head. "Sorry ma'am but once we've processed the scene, no one but investigators are allowed."

She gave the officer a smile and walked away. Michelle walked back to Nick, who was ready to leave. "We need to stay."

Nick looked at her confused. "Why?"

"I found some pictures at the station before we left and they looked like people covered in blood. Then I found that card. Clearly, these are connected and I wanna figure out how."

"But the cops aren't going to let us back in. So unless you can magically teleport in there, we've got to go."

Nick looked behind him and watched as Michelle walked to the side of the house. She snuck around while the cop sat in his car. Nick jogged to catch up with Michelle. She looked around to see if she could find anything outside. She noticed a window open, grabbed onto the windowsill and climbed in. Nick saw her climbing in and poked his head through the window.

"What the hell are you doing?" She shushed him and started looking through Frank and Amelia's things. Nick hoisted himself through the window, knocking over a few things and landing on the ground.

He cursed under his breath and fixed the items that had fallen over. "What exactly are we looking for?"

Michelle shrugged. "Anything that looks suspicious."

Nick threw his hands up. "Ok that helps." He started looking through the closet while Michelle looked through their dresser and side tables. After a few minutes, they found nothing. "Let's look around the house and check the other rooms."

Nick gave her a thumbs up and went to the guest room while she checked what she could get to that wasn't marked as evidence. Nick opened a few drawers and looked through some old boxes but wasn't finding anything. He opened a side table drawer and saw an unmarked envelope. He peeked inside and saw some polaroids. He took them out and started flipping through them.

His stomach dropped and his face felt hot when he noticed they were pictures of Frank, Amelia and other people performing some type of ritual. He couldn't tell what it was or what for but he knew that a few of them looked way too young to be there and that the blood was definitely real. He noticed the girls were barely in their teens. Nick could feel his heart tighten and his blood boil with a strong ringing in his ear.

"Hey did you find anything?"

Michelle's voice snapped him back to reality. Michelle walked into the guest room and she saw the look on Nick's face and could tell something was wrong. "Hey you okay?"

Nick looked at her then back at the pictures. He shook his head and handed the pictures to her. She looked at them and grew more and more furious with each flip of a picture. "Where did you find these?"

Nick pointed to the table. Michelle started to shake and she threw the pictures across the room. Nick picked up the pictures and followed her.

They climbed out through the window and were back outside. Michelle went silent, processing the recent discovery and all the events of the evening. Michelle started to pace back and forth, trying to figure out what to do.

The thought of her bosses, who she had known and respected for years, were now some child murdering cultists. Based on the pictures and how everything looked, they had been doing this for decades.

"How many do you think there were?"

Nick shrugged. "No clue. I only saw eight different girls in the pictures but there might be more pictures."

Michelle continued to pace. "What do we do? Even if we

turn the pictures in to the cops, what are they going to do? The pictures are so old, the girls are definitely dead. No way of telling if any of them survived and who they were."

Nick grabbed Michelle by one of her shoulders. "You've got to slow down, you're making me dizzy."

Michelle stopped pacing and took a deep breath. "We should turn those pictures in. If there are survivors, at least they can try to track down their family members and tell them what happened."

Michelle nodded in agreement and they walked back to the bike. When they got to the police station, they met with the detectives from earlier and explained what happened after everyone had left. One detective rolled his eyes. "You two do realize that you potentially compromised the crime scene, right?"

Michelle and Nick looked at each other and nodded. The detective sighed and finished taking their statement. Michelle handed over the pictures and they were bagged as evidence. "Now go home and stay out of the investigation." Nick gave a thumbs up and they started to walk out of the station.

When they got to the lobby, they noticed two officers bringing in a woman who was covered in blood. She was short, with dark brown hair and brown eyes. Michelle caught a glimpse of the woman's face and gasped.

Nick looked at Michelle then at the woman. "Do you know her?"

Michelle nodded. "That's Travis' girlfriend. Delia!"

Delia looked at Michelle, smiled and began to cry. "I'm finally free."

The two officers took Delia to booking and then she was gone.

Michelle ran over to the officer that took her information. "Hey! Hey! She's a friend of mine! What happened?"

The officer looked at Michelle and then at Delia. "I can't say ma'am but she's definitely not going home tonight."

Michelle walked back over to Nick and they went outside.

"Do you think Delia did something to Travis?"

Michelle shrugged. "It's possible. He was always an asshole to her. I offered my couch to her a few times but she always refused. I guess she finally snapped."

Nick looked across the street and saw a diner. He checked his watch and saw it was ten o'clock. "Hey let's go get something to eat. I dropped the food from earlier at the station so I doubt that stuff is good anymore."

Michelle agreed and they went to cross the street. When Michelle was checking to cross, she saw a black dog watching them and when she looked back the dog was gone.

"Nick, did you see that dog?"

"What dog?"

Michelle pulled Nick as they crossed the street. They barged through the diner's door and Michelle looked through the window to see if the dog was still out there. Nothing but the streetlights and the police station appeared through the window.

Chapter 7

The waitress at the counter greeted them and walked them to a booth. "I'll be back in just a sec for your orders." She gave Nick a flirty look and walked away. Michelle chuckled and looked at the menu.

"You've got a fan," she teased.

Nick looked at her confused. "Who?"

Michelle nodded at the waitress and went back to looking at the menu. Nick looked at the waitress and noticed she was staring at him. Nick turned back in his seat and saw Michelle was trying to hold back her smile.

"Hey, don't be hating on me."

Michelle kept browsing the menu but nothing was sounding good to her. Delia's voice kept echoing inside her head. "Something didn't feel right with Delia."

Nick thought for a moment. "Well you said that Travis was really abusive to her. Maybe she finally snapped, got tired of him beating on her."

Michelle shook her head. "No, that's not like Delia. She's a softie. The woman cries at the end of Disney movies for god's sake."

The waitress came back over and took their orders and handed them in to the cook. Michelle and Nick sat at the table in silence. Nick pulled a pen out of his jacket, a napkin and started drawing.

Michelle watched as Nick sketched the logo.

"Is this close to what it looked like?"

Michelle nodded.

Nick pulled out his phone and took a picture of the napkin. "I've got a cousin who used to know some shady people. They dabbled in some questionable business ethics. Based on that logo, I want to see if he knows who it is." Nick took a picture, texted a message with it and sent it. "Now we wait."

Michelle raised an eyebrow at Nick. "Do you think he would really know this logo?"

Nick shrugged. "I'm not sure. It might be a gang and with those pictures we found. You'd be surprised at how many gangs will fuck someone up if they mess with kids."

A few minutes later, their food came and they started eating. Michelle picked at her food a little bit and then took a bite of the burger. She started to feel sick and ran to the bathroom. Nick got up to go after her but his phone started to ring and he answered. "What's up Danny?"

"Hey I got your message. I didn't recognize it so I asked one of my friends. I haven't heard back from him yet, but now nonna is flipping shit over here. NONNA!! Slow down, I can't translate Italian to English fast enough."

Nick could hear his grandmother talking in the background, switching back and forth from English to Italian. He heard her tell Danny to give her the phone and smack him. "Nicky?!?! Why are you dealing with *magia nera*? Huh!?!"

Michelle walked out of the stall and washed her hands. She splashed some cold water on her face and looked in the mirror. She took a breath and fixed herself up. Her once tan skin now looked pale and sickly. Her green eyes were pale. She felt cold. Michelle walked back to the table and could hear the screaming over the phone.

"*Magia nera?* Nonna what are you talking about?"

"*Magia nera*…the black craft. Who's doing that stuff around you? You need to come and get your rosary."

Nick rolled his eyes. "Nonna, we don't need the rosary. Do you know that symbol?"

"Si, Nicky. That symbol is *demoniaca*."

"What's going on?"

"Ah Nicky, is that a girl? Is she a *strega?*"

"No nonna, she's not a *strega*…at least I don't think she is. She hasn't turned me into a frog yet."

His grandmother started cursing and praying in Italian. "Nicky, *per favore, vieni per una benedizione*."

Nick sighed heavily and looked at Michelle. "Ok, we'll come over after dinner." His grandmother said goodbye and then hung up.

Michelle sat there confused and trying to understand what happened in that conversation. "What just happened?"

Nick rubbed his eyes. "That was my cousin and nonna, my Italian grandmother. She saw the symbol I sent to my cousin and apparently that logo is involved in something demonic. She wants us to come over to get a blessing."

"Is she always like that?"

"Not really, just superstitious. She came from Italy and her family were really into the occult and it scared the shit out of her as a kid. But she remembers a lot of it."

They finished their meal and paid the tab. As they were about to walk out, the jukebox that was silent the entire night kicked on and started playing *The Man Comes Around* by Johnny Cash .

They looked at each other then the waitress, who was just as surprised as them. "Does that always happen?"

The waitress shook her head. "That jukebox hasn't worked in over five years. We've just kept it for decoration."

Michelle and Nick darted out the door and ran for his bike. As they got back to Nick's bike, Michelle watched as a black dog came out from the shadows. She stopped in her tracks and Nick looked at her.

"What are you doing?"

She pointed to the dog and started to shake. "Please tell me you see that too."

Nick looked around but couldn't see what she was pointing at. "There's nothing there."

Michelle's heart started to race and beat hard against her chest. She felt sweaty and started to feel sick again. She dropped to her knees and groaned in pain.

"Michelle, you ok?"

Michelle whimpered and shook her head. "We need to go."

Nick scooped her up and buckled her to him. Nick revved the bike on and sped off down the road.

Chapter 8

Nick and Michelle arrived at a red brick duplex apartment. Nick got off the bike and helped Michelle off.

"This is my grandmother's house. I told her we would come here after dinner. There was no way of getting out of that."

"Are you still feeling bad? Do we need to go to a doctor?"

"No, I'm ok. I think it's just that stress of everything and then trying to force myself to eat just made me sick. I'm good though. Thank you."

They walked up the stairs and before Nick could knock on the door, it flew open and a short thin woman with silver curly hair was there greeting them. "Thank god you're finally here, Nicky. I was starting to get worried. Come in, come, come."

Inside, Danny was waiting on the couch. They gave each other a wave. "Nonna, this is Michelle. She works at the radio station where I'm helping out tonight. Michelle, this is my nonna and that's my cousin, Danny." Michelle nodded a greeting. Danny gave Nick a smirk and nod of approval.

Nonna smiled at Michelle and pinched her cheek. "Oh, Michelle. *Lei è molta bella.* You may call me Janet." Michelle smiled and shook Janet's hand.

"Thank you, Janet. I don't want to take too much of your time so I'll cut to the chase. Danny and Nick said that you recognize that symbol that was on the business card I found."

Janet nodded and led them to the dining table. "Yes, please sit." She poured them coffee and gave them some pastries. "I recognize that symbol from my childhood." Nick looked at his grandmother surprised.

"Really?"

She nodded. "Yes. There was a man who came to my friend's grandfather's shop. They were business partners for a while and then her grandfather angered the man. The next time they saw her grandfather, he was dead in his home. They said some animal got in and killed him. But there were two girls that had gone missing at the same time. I was barely ten years old and they weren't that much older then me."

Janet rubbed her hands together anxiously as she recalled everything from the families searching the woods, guards looking in houses and investigating potential leads but the attempts left them in dead ends. The mother of one of the girls would sit outside the front door to watch the streets. Days turned into weeks, then months, then years.

By the time Janet left the village, the families had either moved on or died of grief. She recalled that when the wife of the shop owner was on her deathbed, a man had stopped by to visit her. A few minutes later, she passed away.

"But that man was not from our village. He was a demon. That symbol was his, he left it branded in the grandfather's shop and another shop owner who died the same way."

Michelle sat back and thought for a moment. She remembered the pictures and how it looked like some ritual they were doing. "Did her grandfather do some kind of ritual? Or hurt anyone?"

Janet thought for a moment then nodded. "It was never

proven but we all knew he had done something."

"What makes you think that the man that helped the grandfather was a demon? Maybe he was just a businessman that was actually helping the grandfather."

Janet shook her head. "No, because I saw him in the shop one time and his eyes glowed… and he had a big black dog with him. It was dead but alive. Rotting, fresh out of a grave."

Michelle gasped and her eyes grew wide when Janet mentioned the dog.

"Have *you* seen the black dog?" Janet asked, grabbing Michelle's hand.

Michelle nodded.

"Nonna, come on. A demon man making deals? Rotting dogs? Is he like the *babau* you would threaten to call if I didn't eat my vegetables when I was a kid?"

Janet looked at Nick and shook her head. "No Nicky, that was to frighten a small boy into getting his nutrition. This is serious." Janet got up and walked to the fridge. She grabbed two eggs and filled two cups with water and salt.

Nick and Danny saw what she had and rolled their eyes.

"Oh god, not the eggs."

Janet smacked Nick on the shoulder and made him stand up. She ran the egg along his arms, shoulders, head, down both his legs, and across his chest. She cracked the egg into the cup of salt water and there was clear water and healthy yolk. She patted him on the shoulder and he sat back down.

Janet motioned for Michelle to stand up and repeated the process. When she cracked the egg, the cup filled with black and red liquid. They watched in horror as the liquid started to bubble and boil over the cup, staining the white lace tablecloth. Michelle fell back in her chair, horrified. Janet hugged her.

"It's ok, *mia cara*. You are a good person. This is just showing that something evil is attached to you, but we can break it." Janet walked into another room and gathered some supplies.

Michelle's foot started to shake and bounce. Nick held Michelle's hand and gave it a gentle squeeze of encouragement.

She took a shaky breath and regained control of herself just as her phone started vibrating. It was Derek calling her. She stepped away from the table and answered.

"Hey what's up?"

"Are you guys playing a prank? Is everything ok?"

Michelle was confused. "Yeah, why?"

"I was listening to the show and it cut to someone screaming. I tried calling the cops but they wouldn't answer. When I drove down here, I heard a woman screaming inside the station. Are you here? There's no way I'm going in unless this is just a sick final night prank."

Michelle looked at Nick. "No, we're not at the station. We had to leave. What else is goin' on?"

"Then who…? I'm not sure, but the door was wide open when I got here and…"

Derek went quiet and Michelle could hear a woman talking in the background.

"Michelle? If you're fucking with me, this isn't funny."

There was static and a thud. Derek groaned and screamed in pain. The line went dead.

"Derek! Derek!" Michelle stuffed her phone back in her pocket. "We have to go back!" She stood up and grabbed Nick's arm.

"Hey what's going on?"

"Derek is at the station. Something is attacking him. We need to go now."

"Danny, call the cops!"

Michelle and Nick ran back outside, climbed on the bike and rode off.

Janet came back to the dining room and saw that Nick and Michelle left.

"Danny! Where did Nick and Michelle go?"

Dan was already dialing the police. "Michelle got a call and they ran out. Looked like an emergency."

Janet rolled her eyes and raised smacked her sides in frustration. "Dammit Danny! Michelle is cursed and you just let her leave. The girl is in danger!"

The radio in the living room kicked on and started playing *Hotel California.* Janet and Dan looked at each other. Janet walked over to the radio, picked it up and threw it outside. She made the cross with her chest and walked back inside, slamming the door behind her.

Chapter 9

Vince Rails sat in the shadows underneath the busy highway bridge. He bundled himself up to hide from any cars that might've taken the route under the bridge. Winds coming from the highway brushed against him, causing him to bundle up more.

"Hello Vince."

Vince was startled by a female voice. He looked beside him and saw a pale woman with black hair staring at him.

"Lamia! What are you doing here?"

Lamia smiled. "Well Vince, since you've technically been living under a rock I'll give you the heads up. The station has gone down and we've come to collect."

Vince looked at her confused as a black limousine pulled around.

"Oh come on, why should I have to go? Frank and Travis started all that shit and now I have to pay? That's bullshit!"

Lamia shrugged. "Not my problem, Vince. You, Lexi and Travis participated in the ritual, and to be quite honest, you were the one that seemed to enjoy it a lot more than the others."

Vince started to shake and smack his head.

Lamia grabbed his hand. "Don't make this harder. I really don't want to have to work up a sweat at the end of the night."

Vince got up and then made a run for the highway. Lamia raised her hand, causing a force to hit Vince and make him fall flat on his face. He groaned in pain as he rolled over on his back. Lamia stood over him and glared at him.

"I tried to warn you Vince."

Vince looked up at Lamia and spat at her. "Fuck you."

Lamia could feel some spit on her face and she wiped it off.

"Seriously Vince? This is what we've resorted to?"

Vince struggled to get up while Lamia grabbed him by his leg and dragged him to the limo. He screamed and begged for her to let him go. He kicked at her a few times but failed in every attempt.

The back door of the limo slowly opened and the tune of *Hotel California* echoed from its radio.

"Got to hand it to you Vince, the station always did play some good music."

Vince tried to hold on to the concrete but the pain from Lamia dragging him to the car started to get to him and he finally gave in. She picked him up by his shirt collar and shoved him into the backseat and slammed the door behind him.

Vince quickly shot up in the seat and desperately tried to open the door, even kicking it and the window but to no avail.

The air in the backseat was heavy and smelt of cigar tobacco. Vince coughed and noticed there was a man sitting in the shadows. The man struck a match, lit his cigar and blew out the match.

"Vince, it's a pleasure to see you again after all this time. You look well."

Vince swallowed hard, his heart beating fast and his throat felt tight.

"Mason..."

Mason smirked and nodded.

"I'm surprised you remember me after all this time. What's it been? Thirty odd years? How have you been?"

Vince looked at himself in his tattered clothes. "Been better. I guess the station went to shit after I left."

Mason shrugged as he took a puff off his cigar and blew the smoke at Vince. "More or less, which brings me to our business for the evening."

Mason snapped his fingers and a black puff of smoke swirled next to Mason and started to take the shape of a black dog with red eyes.

The stench of rotting flesh hit Vince's nose and he started to choke, throwing up a little on the limo's floor. Mason rolled his eyes as he patted the dog on its head.

"Oh come on now, it's not that bad. I can only assure you it's worse compared to where you're going."

Vince looked at Mason and the dog while wiping the vomit from his mouth.

"Why me? I didn't sign that stupid contract. Why do I have to pay for Frank and Travis' bullshit?"

Mason looked at Vince and raised an eyebrow.

"*Oh contraire mon frère,* as I recall, **YOU** were very active in the rituals. Hell, I think more than half the girls that were selected were brought in by you."

Vince leaned forward, hung his head and started to sob.

Mason grimaced at Vince's crying and handed him a box of tissues.

"Now Vince, you had to have known that there was a price to pay for everything."

Vince continued to sob, tears rolling down his eyes and snot dribbling from his nose. Mason rolled his eyes as he grabbed a bottle of McCellan '67 and two glasses from the mini bar. He poured some into each glass and offered one to Vince.

"Last call, Vinny boy."

Vince looked at the glass then snatched the bottle from the mini bar.

"If I'm gonna burn, I'm going to at least warm up first."

Mason smirked and sipped from the glass.

Vince sat in silence, considering the possibility that this might actually be the end for him. Then, an idea came to him.

"Wait, what if WE make a deal?"

Mason raised an eyebrow at the suggestion and chuckled.

"Vinny, do I look like Howie Mandel? Do you see a whole bunch of ladies with little briefcases? You have nothing to offer."

"And that means I have nothing to lose."

Mason looked Vince up and down. He could tell by the look in Vince's eyes that he was desperate for his freedom.

"Go on."

"In the contract, Frank and Travis had to do favors and stuff and as long as it was fulfilled everything was good. Right?"

Mason thought for a moment and nodded. "To an extent and to my recollection, yes that was in the original deal."

Vince sighed with relief.

"The new host, Michelle, didn't perform any of the rituals but Frank still let her be host. It's not fair that she gets a free pass. What if she takes my place and I'll do whatever you want me to. I'll go around and collect people like Lamia and Jack. Or I'll pick up hellhound shit. I don't care, I just don't want to die."

Mason thought for a moment about the offer and smiled.

"Enticing."

Mason tapped on the visor window and it rolled halfway down.

"Benny boy, take us to the station. We'll be paying Michelle a visit."

Benny gave Mason a thumbs up and the glass went back up.

Mason looked back at Vince, who was still sipping on the whiskey bottle.

"So do we have a deal?" Vince asked, wiping his mouth.

Mason extended his hand out to Vince. "I believe we do, Mr. Vince."

Chapter 10

Nick and Michelle got back to the station and looked around. There was no sign of Derek, cops or any signs of distress.

"Where is he?" Nick asked, checking the alley and dumpsters around the station.

"I don't know. He said he was here, and that someone that looked like me was inside."

"Should we wait till the cops get here? If someone hurt Derek, then they might still be here."

A deafening wail came from inside the station, calling Michelle's name.

"Oh my god, that's Derek!"

Michelle ran for the door but Nick grabbed her before she could open it.

"Michelle, STOP! It has to be a set up."

Michelle glared at Nick as another scream came from inside, shoved him away and ran inside. The heavy metal door slammed behind her. Nick ran up to it and pulled as hard as he could but it didn't budge. It was locked.

"Shit."

Inside, Michelle found the lobby trashed. Blood splattered the wall and shreds of fabric were scattered around the room.

She searched the lobby for any sign of Derek until she saw a trail of blood going down the hall to the other office area.

She could hear Nick banging on the lobby door.

"Michelle! Open the door!"

He banged a couple more times but she didn't respond.

Instead, Michelle slowly walked down the hall to Frank's office, and grabbed a letter opener off the desk before she cautiously followed the trail further.

It led to a closed door she had never been through. She opened the office door and the first thing she saw was a bloody Derek in the middle of the room laying on his back.

"Oh my god."

Derek looked at her and started to weep.

"Michelle."

He reached out for her as she knelt down beside him.

"Derek, I'm so sorry. I'm so sorry. Who did this to you?"

Derek waved his hand and just held her.

"Michelle, it's ok. Not…your…fault. I was just scared…about you…being hurt."

Michelle grabbed her phone and went to dial 911 but saw it had died.

"FUCK!!!"

Michelle threw her phone across the room and screamed out of anger. Derek coughed as he tried to speak. Michelle held his hand and saw huge gashes across his arms and chest and a bite mark on his leg. They appeared to have come from a large dog. She knew deep down, he wasn't going to make it down the hall.

Michelle sobbed.

"Who did this?"

Michelle jumped as a loud bang and some footsteps came running down the hall, and was relieved when Nick appeared in the doorway, panting.

Derek started to hyperventilate and pulled at Michelle urgently.

Michelle looked from Nick to Derek and saw nothing but fear in Derek's eyes.

"Derek, it's ok. I need you to calm down. Nick isn't going to hurt you. He's good."

Derek shook his head and pulled Michelle close to him.

"No…HE did this to me."

Michelle looked back at Nick as Derek went entirely limp and gave out his last breath.

Michelle wailed as she held her friend in her arms and rocked back and forth, cradling his body.

Nick walked over and placed his hand on Michelle's shoulder.

Michelle fiercely brushed it off as she shoved Nick away.

"WHAT THE HELL DID YOU DO?!?!"

She shoved him to the ground and Nick looked at her confused.

"What are you talking about?"

Michelle grabbed her letter opener from her pocket and pointed it at Nick.

"WHOA! WHOA! WHOA! Wait a sec, you can't possibly believe I did any of this."

Michelle got on top of Nick and started punching him.

"You son of a bitch!"

She punched him over and over.

Nick grabbed both of her hands, shoved her off and pinned her down.

"Michelle, STOP! How could I have done this while we were at my grandma's and when we got here. We've been together all night, it's physically impossible for me to have done this."

"Damn, I almost had you."

Michelle and Nick looked over and saw Derek standing up, smiling at them.

Nick got off of Michelle and they stood up.

"Derek?"

Derek took a bow and chuckled.

"Not quite." He snapped his fingers and *Total Eclipse of the Heart* started playing on the speakers.

Michelle and Nick stared at Derek, who's face slowly became blurry and shifted into another man. Michelle felt sick to her stomach.

"Who the hell are you?"

"Won't matter, but for the time being, the name is Jack."

Jack checked his watch.

"Mason should be here with the others in a couple of minutes. I think we have some room for a little playtime."

Jack looked over at Nick and winked at him. Nick could feel his throat start to tighten and close. He gasped for air as he dropped to knees.

Michelle grabbed Nick's hand but Jack shoved her back, causing her to fly across the room and over a desk.

She groaned and tried to pull herself up but her back hurt with each movement.

Nick gasped for breath, his vision started to blur and his face felt hot.

Michelle grabbed a stapler that had fallen from the desk and threw it straight into Jack's face. There was a satisfying crunch, and the sound of him groaning made Michelle chuckle a little.

"Got you, fucker."

Jack glared at Michelle and his grip from Nick was released. Jack wiped his nose and his entire hand was covered in blood.

"You bitch."

He lunged over to Michelle and picked her up by her shirt. She grabbed a hold of his arm and kicked him in the groin. He dropped her as he fell to the ground.

Michelle limped over to Nick and helped him up.

They limped and dragged each other down the hallway back to the front. As soon as they reached the lobby, the front doors flew open. Michelle squinted to look through the dimly lit room and she could barely make out one of the figures that walked in.

"Vince? Is that you?"

Vince had a guilty, sad expression..

"Yeah it's me kiddo."

Michelle looked at the other man, who just looked back at her..

"Who's that?" Michelle asked, still helping Nick stand on his feet.

Mason smiled softly as he approached Michelle.

"You must be Michelle. Vince has told me some *interesting* things about you on the way here."

Michelle raised an eyebrow and glanced over at Vince, who was just shamefully looking down at his feet.

"And what things has Vince told you?"

Mason looked over at Vince.

"Vince, would you like to inform Michelle of what you told me in the car?"

Vince swallowed hard and cleared his throat.

"I told Mason that you were a druggy and you stole from the radio station. You also didn't perform the ritual like we had to."

Michelle glared at Vince. She dropped Nick, charged at Vince and punched him.

"You lying son of a bitch! If anyone is a druggy thief it's your pathetic ass."

Mason curiously raised an eyebrow.

"Vince, is this true? Are you lying? Because you know how much I hate lying."

Vince looked from Michelle to Mason and nodded as he started to sob.

Mason rolled his eyes as he gave Vince a handkerchief. Vince took it and blew his nose with it.

"Michelle, if you follow me, I believe we have some business to discuss."

Michelle looked at Mason confused.

"Business? What kind of business?"

Mason smiled softly and nodded.

"You'll see soon. Please, follow me."

Michelle watched Mason walk to the office and helped Nick back up. She looked back at Vince and slapped him. She helped Nick walk to the office.

Mason looked back at Vince and grinned at him, snapping his fingers. Vince heard a growling sound next to him and saw a black dog with red eyes snarling. The dog leapt onto Vince and started tearing into him, his screams echoing through the station.

Chapter 11

Mason closed the door behind him and Vince's screams became muffled. Michelle helped Nick into a chair and helped him get comfortable.

"Now, Michelle. Let's get down to it."

Mason walked over to Frank's desk and sat in his chair. He grabbed his cigarette holder from his pocket, put one in between his lips and lit it with a golden dragon lighter. He offered one to Michelle and Nick but they declined. Mason shrugged and placed the case back into his pocket.

"So, since Vince is disposed of at the moment…" There was a thud at the door with a bloody hand print dragged across the window and the sound of a dog playfully growling could be heard in the hallway. "Let's talk business."

Michelle sat in a chair next to Nick.

"I told you I'm not doing business with you. I don't want any part of this."

Mason nodded. "Yeah, I know, but that's not why I'm here. I'm here because Mr. Kibbles and Bits out there tried to sell you out and I don't tolerate that."

Michelle and Nick looked at each other confused, then back at Mason.

"Um, ok."

Mason raised an eyebrow. "You seem confused."

Michelle nodded.

"Well, yeah. You're a demon, you're supposed to influence people and make people sell their souls, collect sacrifices and shit."

Mason chuckled.

"Yeah, there's always that stereotype. A bit bigoted to be honest but I can understand the confusion."

Michelle shook her head, trying to process what she just heard.

Nick sat up in his chair and leaned forward.

"What the fuck are you talking about?"

Mason rolled his eyes.

"What I'm trying to tell you is that I didn't make anyone do anything that they didn't want to do. Frank and I made a deal. He signed a contract for fame but he didn't follow the rules, so either way he and everyone who participated had to pay the price."

"But you told him they had to kill people to do all that."

Mason reached into his other pocket, pulled out the contract and handed it to Michelle.

"Please show me where it says they had a gun to their head and were forced to kill people," Mason said. He took a drag from his cigarette.

Michelle looked through the contract, but all she could find was a section mentioning: *a favor needed to be fulfilled annually and collected.*

"What's this favor that needed to be done?"

Mason chuckled.

"To be honest, we left it open ended. It could've been anything from bathing a hellhound to just buying a simple bag of chips.

We never specified because we wanted to see what was worth giving up. However, when this certain deal was made it was at the peak of Satanic Panic so I could understand that there was some confusion about the terms and conditions."

Michelle sat there and glared at Mason.

"And it never occurred to you to reveal that information at any point during that time that wasn't what you meant by a favor?"

Mason shook his head.

"Nope. It just showed what they would've given for their fame. They sacrificed so many girls and in so many ways. It honestly made it easier for when the end came. There wouldn't be any negotiations or trials for redemption. Just straight down the broken escalator to the big man downstairs."

Michelle started to feel sick.

"If I was you Michelle, I'd consider myself lucky. You worked here. You busted your ass and became a host. You didn't have to sell yourself. Hell, I'm surprised they didn't sacrifice *you* to us."

Nick thought about everything.

"So, what? They did it all because they wanted to? And Satan is an advocate for anti-child abuse and the death penalty."

Mason took a final drag from his cigarette and put it out on Frank's contract.

"In so many words, yes, you could say that."

"But they still didn't deserve to die. They're shitty people for sure but they didn't deserve to die."

Mason leaned back in his chair.

"That always amuses me. You humans do bad shit and try to make excuses for it. That's why we make the deals. You do fucked up shit, you get fucked up consequences. Frank and company already had some darkness in them. All that contract did was bring it to the surface, show who they truly were and then when it was time, we came to collect."

"So you expect us to believe you? How do we know that you didn't give us some bullshit paper?"

Mason raised an eyebrow and got up from the chair.

"Listen, I have far more important things to worry about. Now, if you don't want to believe everything that you have seen in front of you, that's fine. But if you let me *show* you, then maybe it'll put some things in perspective for you."

Michelle and Nick looked at each other.

"How are you going to show us?"

Mason walked around the desk to Michelle and held out his hand. Michelle looked at it cautiously then at Nick, who shrugged at her. She looked at Mason's hand and grabbed it.

Nick sat there as he watched Michelle and Mason flicker and fade out.

"Oh no it's fine, I'll just stay here with the damn dog and make sure he doesn't destroy anything else."

<u>1986</u>

Michelle and Mason appear in Frank's office. Michelle looked around the now tidy and organized office. There's fresh wallpaper and the tiled floors are clean and unscuffed.

"What the hell? This is Frank's office. Where's Nick?"

"Well, since this is 1986, I would imagine he's probably just a twinkle in his daddy's eye right now."

Michelle looked at Mason.

"1986? How the in the hell are we in 1986?!?!"

"You wanted to know if your people were honest and good

as you thought they were, and here we are. A year and day after the contract was made. This is the night we came to collect the very first favor."

Michelle looked around and saw a calendar on the desk, marking it June 13 1986.

"So demons can time travel?"

Mason chuckled.

"I fuckin' wish. Do you know how much we would clean house with in gambling and politics? No, this is just a flashback."

Mason checked his watch.

"Ooo… we better hurry to the party."

He walked over to the office door and opened it, motioning Michelle to follow him. She cautiously followed him as they walked down the hall.

They walked down to the other office area. There was a mixture of voices chattering to each other, whispering. Mason got to the office door and looked back at Michelle.

"You sure you still want to watch this?"

Michelle nodded.

Mason shrugged and tapped on the door.

It slowly opened and a young Frank peered through the dim room.

"Hey, Mason."

Frank appeared on edge, jittery, heavy dark circles under his eyes. Amelia was by a desk, chewing on her nails while Travis sat next to a young lady who seemed not all there and possibly under the influence. Mason walked through the door.

"Amelia, Travis, you two look well. How are you?"

Travis got up from the couch while the girl remained motionless on the couch.

"Hey man, we're good. We've got you something."

Travis nudged the young woman, who barely reacted.

"Sorry, she drank too much so she's a little out of it."

Travis smacked the girl on her cheek a few times to wake her up. Michelle watched her steps as she walked more into the room.

Mason saw her walking in out of the corner of his eye.

"Don't worry. This is a flashback, nothing will change if you touch anything."

Michelle pushed herself against a wall to avoid being seen, even though no one even acknowledged her presence.

Travis picked up the girl and shook her.

The girl whimpered as he slapped her on the head.

"Man, I told you we shouldn't have given her so much."

Frank walked over to the girl. "Doesn't matter, she's for Mason anyway."

Amelia grew more on edge and ran out of the room. Michelle watched as Amelia as she ran past her. Travis and Frank ripped the girl's clothes off and threw her at Mason.

"Here. Here's your 'favor.'" Travis said, throwing clothes on the floor.

Mason smirked, acting to be impressed. He examined the girl's face. He could tell by her eyes she was barely in her teens.

"What's your name?"

"Clara." The girl whimpered.

Mason brushed the hair out the girl's face, and laid her down on the couch. Mason could tell the drugs in her system were already taking her, she didn't have much longer.

"So, Clara is your offering?"

"Well yeah, isn't that what you want?"

"Is a life what you're willing to give?"

Travis and Frank looked at each other.

"If that's what it takes to seal the deal, then yeah."

Mason shrugged. "Then so be it. The favor is claimed. What you do with her now is entirely at your discretion."

Mason walked out with Michelle right behind him.

The screams of Clara echoed through the hallway. Michelle went to the door and tried to open it but it was locked. She banged on the door but it wouldn't budge.

"You bastards! OPEN THE DOOR!! Don't you hurt her!!"

Chapter 12

Michelle screamed as she fell back into her chair, landing in her seat with a hard thud. Nick shot up from his seat and approached her.

"Hey what happened?"

Mason sat in his chair, waiting for Michelle to calm down. She looked at Mason and started to sob. Everything was true. Frank, Amelia and Travis did everything Mason said they had done. Without force, without threat, without remorse.

"Mason's right. About everything, he was right."

Mason shrugged in a 'I told you so' way.

"Well then what happens to us? I didn't participate in the ritual and Nick is just a temp from a different station. Where does that leave us?"

"Well, you two can either keep running the station or get rid of it. You guys are not bound to this place in any way. I just came here because Vince made a deal, failed miserably and I wanted to clear some shit up."

Mason checked his watch. "Damn, night's already over, I must dash. You two kids behave yourself now."

Mason snapped his fingers and the overhead speakers crackled. The song *Mama, I'm coming home* started playing. The sun started to peek through the office window. Mason slowly started to become translucent and smoke started to surround him. He lowered his glasses, his brown eyes quickly became a fiery ember color and he winked at Nick and Michelle.

"See you around kiddies."

The smoke dispersed and he was gone.

Nick and Michelle sat there in confusion and fear.

"What the actual fuck?"

Michelle shrugged.

"Dude, I have no idea."

Nick helped Michelle out of her chair and they left the office. The dog was gone but its footprints and leftover carnage from Vince was still there.

They walked outside and were greeted by the morning sun.

"So what should we do now?"

Nick looked around. Still no officers or any sign of anyone was around them.

"I don't know, I thought this place would've been surrounded by cops or something."

Nick pulled out phone and noticed he had a bunch of calls and texts from his grandmother and cousin.

"Oh shit."

Nick called his grandmother, who immediately answered and started cussing him out.

"Nonna, I'm sorry. We were dealing with this. I didn't hear my phone go off."

Michelle could barely make out what Janet was saying but she knew she was mad and took the phone from Nick.

"Hey Janet, it's Michelle."

"Oh sweetie, thank goodness you're ok. I was so worried. Dan had called the police but when they went to the station and saw that no one was there they thought it was a prank call.

Then when Nick wouldn't answer his phone, I got scared, but I am glad you two are ok. Come over and I'll make you breakfast."

Michelle chuckled.

"Ok we'll be over later."

They said goodbye and hung up.

Michelle handed Nick his phone and he put it in his pocket.

"I don't know what you did to my nonna, but she loves you. I guarantee she'll have you in her will by the end of the week."

Michelle laughed as she looked back at the studio. Her heart sank at the thought of how many girls died for a bunch of people who thought it would make them famous. She felt ashamed for working there and being affiliated with them.

"God, I don't know what to do now. This place was like a second home. I got to do a lot of cool things here and play music. Now that I know about everything that happened, I'm just hurting now."

Nick wrapped his arm around Michelle and pulled her close.

"You'll be alright. But we should definitely call the cops and tell them something happened here. Not sure what, but we'll make it up as we go."

Nick called the cops and told them about the radio station being destroyed and they needed to make a report.

Police arrived and swarmed the area. The officers that walked inside and one immediately got sick.

The detectives took Nick and Michelle's statements: Two radio hosts were working their last show. The equipment started acting up and decided to close shop early. Nick forgot something and came back, noticed all the blood and damage.

Vince's corpse couldn't be identified and Michelle acted like she didn't know him. The officer's told them that they were ok to leave but to stay close in case of further investigations. Nick and Michelle gave the officers their information and left.

"Hey can you take me home real quick so I can get cleaned up?"

Nick obliged the request and took Michelle home.

She entered her apartment and cleaned herself. When she was walking out, she saw Derek heading out too.

"Oh hey! I listened to the last show but it went off air early. What happened?"

"Equipment issues. But it doesn't matter anymore, the station is over and done with. The owners were shitty people and I'm glad it's over."

Her response surprised Derek.

"Oh, well I'm glad you won't have to deal with that anymore. So what are you going to do now?"

Michelle shrugged.

"Not sure but I'll figure something out."

Michelle returned to Nick and the bike.

"You ready? Because nonna keeps asking when we'll be over."

"I'm ready. Let's get over there before she sends the search party."

Nick revved the bike's engine as Michelle climbed on. She put on her helmet and rode.

They pulled up to Janet's apartment building. As they approached the front door, it flew open and Janet was waiting there.

"You two are just in time! Come, come."

Nick and Michelle smiled as they entered.

Dan sat at the dining table reading the newspaper while Nick and Michelle sat down.

"See you two survived the night."

Nick nodded.

"Yep. Alive and everything is still attached."

Janet walked in carrying a platter of pancakes and fruit. There were muffins on the table and fresh eggs.

"Go on, start digging in while it's hot."

Everyone started making their plates while Janet brought in more food then sat down.

"So what happened after you left? We tried to call so many times and we got worried."

Nick and Michelle looked at each other.

Michelle took a deep breath and told Janet everything that happened at the studio: Vince trying to kill Michelle, Mason and him showing Michelle the first collection, the cops finally coming and talking to them.

"Oh my goodness. So that's it? The studio is closed and everything?"

Michelle nodded as she took a bite from a pancake.

"Yep. The studio is closed forever. No more of *The Lair*."

They continued their breakfast in silence. Nick sat there and picked at a piece of his food.

"It really sucks that it ended the way it did. You did a really awesome job as the host."

Michelle smiled and shrugged.

"That's just show biz. It comes and goes."

Nick shook his head.

"What if we did a podcast about the studio?"

Michelle looked at him confused.

"What are you talking about?"

"Think about it. Everyone loves haunted places and scary stories. What if we started our own podcast? We can take callers' stories and talk about them. Our first show can be about what happened at the studio and go from there."

Michelle thought about it.

"I don't know. It's way too soon and I'm not even sure if I want to be anywhere near a radio or mix board any time soon."

"Well of course not right now but when things do get settled down we should definitely do something like that."

"I'll sleep on it."

They continued their breakfast and talked more about the previous night's events.

After their meal, Michelle went home and tried to sleep. She could feel her phone buzzing. She groaned and looked at the called ID: Jackie.

Jackie was her cousin from Texas. They were more sisters than anything.

She answered the phone.

"Hey Jax. What's up?"

"Hey Mickey. Haven't heard from you in awhile and just wanted to see how you were."

Michelle sighed.

"Been better. Last night was my final night on air so now I'm just at home trying to sleep. What have you been up to?"

Jackie sighed softly, like she had been crying. Michelle could tell something was off but wasn't sure what it was.

"Jax, are you ok?"

"Yeah I'm fine. James and I have just hit a rough patch and have been fighting recently."

Michelle sat up in bed and pressed the facetime button on her phone. Jackie declined.

"Jackie, did he hit you?"

Jackie sniffled.

"No."

"Jackie..."

Jackie sniffled again.

"Yes."

Michelle sighed.

"Do I need to come get you? Do you need anything?"

"No, I'll be fine. I have a meeting with a lawyer in a few days to talk about the divorce. I just wanted to talk to you and see how you were doing."

"I'm ok but you let me know if you need anything and I'll come running."

Jackie chuckled.

"I know and that's why I love you girl. Hey, now that you're done with that station, maybe you can start your own gig."

Michelle shrugged.

"You know that's what my coworker said. I wasn't sure because of everything that happened with the station. I'm still thinking about it."

"You should do it. I always liked the scary stories you used to tell."

"I'll think about it."

The girls said goodbye and hung up.

Michelle laid back in bed. She looked at her phone again and pulled up Nick's phone number and texted him: *You win. The show must go on.*

Chapter 13

<u>Four Months Later: Halloween</u>

Nick adjusted the mics as Michelle checked the recording station.

"You ready?" Nick asked as he adjusted in the chair and organized his notes.

Michelle nodded.

"I think so. I hope we get some good stories tonight."

"I think we will. People loved our story about the radio station from hell. I don't see why anyone wouldn't like our scary shit." He made air quote motions with his fingers when he said the word story.

Michelle chuckled as she checked her watch.

"Almost six o'clock. Let's fuck this chicken."

Nick smiled as he flipped the light on and turned on the mics. He pointed to Michelle, giving her the ok to start.

"Good evening, my little late night parasites. It's the night mother like no other, Skully Riot. It is all Hallow's Eve and the dead are out and about so be careful. We have classic rock and some spooky stories to tell you. If you have any stories to share, give us a shout from the beyond and we'll share it on air. Dig you guys up in a few!"

They switched to some Halloween music as they started

receiving messages in their chat.

Between songs, Nick and Michelle took turns reading the viewers' stories and answering calls. By the time eleven-thirty rolled around, they had read through most of the stories and were now finishing up with a Halloween trivia game.

"First one to call in and tell us Ash's full name from *Evil Dead* and bonus points if you can give us the nickname. Winner gets a $200 prize, a special shout out and they get to pick the final song of the night. Sorry, we're going to make you guys work for this one. Good luck."

A few callers came in and gave them answers but none were close. As it got closer to midnight, none of the callers were getting it. Michelle answered the last call.

"Alright caller, give us your answer."

"Ashley Joann Williams, aka Ashy Slashy."

Michelle and Nick looked at each other.

"Well congrats, you unlucky caller, you won! Prize is still $200 and now you get to pick the last song of the night. What shall it be?"

The caller took a shaky breath and exhaled.

"*Sister Christian* by Night Rider."

"And what's your name?"

"Jackie."

Michelle thought for a moment. The voice sounded familiar. She checked the phone number that popped up on screen. It was Jackie, her cousin.

"Ok Miss Jackie, here's your song for the night and I'm going to grab your info to send you that sweet money. Hold tight."

Michelle hit the mute button on her mic and pulled out her phone. She saw six missed calls and ten texts from Jackie. Michelle called her.

Jackie quickly answered.

"Hello?"

"Jax, are you ok?"

Jackie sniffled.

"Yeah, I'm fine. Uh James and I finally divorced. I guess he got tired of me telling him no. I'm also not sure if you heard, but grams passed away earlier today."

Michelle's heart dropped.

"What? What happened?"

Jackie sniffled again.

"Not sure. I just got a call from her lawyer earlier this evening. I haven't gotten a chance to call you because I've been packing. She left us the house and some other things. If it's ok with you, I'd like to move into the house. After the divorce with James, I don't have anything and need somewhere to go."

Michelle nodded.

"No, of course. You need that place more than I do and he won't know where you live so you'll be so much safer there. Do you need help with anything?"

"Uh, I was actually going to ask if you wanted to move in with me. I don't wanna be in that old house by myself but I know you still have the radio stuff and I didn't want to take you away from there."

"Girl, I'll pack my shit and be down there in a few days. I'll call you when I'm down there. Be safe getting there."

"Will do. I'll see you soon."

Michelle looked at Nick, who sat there confused.

"Everything ok?"

"No, that was my cousin Jax. She just called me and told me our grams had passed away. She also just got out of a shitty relationship and wants me to go down there."

Nick leaned back in his chair.

"Oh shit. How long do you need off?"

Michelle shrugged.

"Not sure, but I'll figure that stuff out later. Let's finish tonight and I'll plan it out when I get home."

Midnight came and they closed for the night. They grabbed their things and started heading home.

Later, in her apartment, Michelle started making a list of everything she would need for her trip. There was a loud thud at her bedroom window and it caused her to jump back.

CAW!

She opened the blinds to see a black bird staring at her. She cautiously examined the bird.

"Can I help you?"

The bird tilted its head, dropped something on her window seal and flew off. She took the item and quickly realized it was an old key. Outside, the bird was nowhere in sight.

"What the hell?"

She closed the window and locked it. She sat on her bed and examined the key closer. She noticed some small engravings in the key. On closer inspection she realized the engravings were of crosses with a small canine skull in the middle.

Her laptop lit up and started playing *House of the Rising Sun* by The Animals.

"You've got to be fucking kidding me."

Coming Soon: Feral

Ben Davis sat on his back porch, listening to the echoing sound of the summer cicadas that surrounded his house. He watched the sun start to drift into the tree line, slowly starting to disappear behind the trees, the Texas heat dying with it and small gentle breezes brushed against his sun aged skin.

He closed his eyes in serenity when static from his radio blasted through the speaker, causing him to almost jump out of his chair and spill his beer. He cursed under his breath and went to the radio. Just as he was about to turn the radio off, the song "Evil Woman" by The Eagles started playing. He stared at the radio in confusion and turned it off. He heard a whistle behind him and turned.

He saw a woman coming out from the wood line, no more than 18 years old, with straw colored hair and a red winter coat covered in dirt and mud. She appeared to be making her way to his porch, like she was coming home after a rough day. He watched in wonder and fixed his glasses, staring at her as she kept walking and getting closer. "Tilly," he said under his breath.

The girl stopped in her tracks, looked at him and tilted her head as if she could hear him from the other side of the acre. Ben watched her in awe until a car horn startled him in his driveway. His head snapped back, and he saw his neighbor Henry Williams making his way towards the porch. Ben looked back at the girl, but she had vanished.

"Sorry for scaring ya, Benny," Henry chuckled. "Couldn't help myself, hadn't seen ya in a while and wanted to check in." They shook hands and hugged.

"I'm doing alright, just been trying to keep myself busy this time of year," Ben smiled, trying to convince Henry that he was alright but failing miserably. Henry placed a hand on Ben's shoulder and gave him a knowing pat as if to say, 'I know you're not.'

"Yeah, yeah, I know," Henry said. Ben walked back to his chair and sat down, Henry following suit in the chair next to him. Ben slumped forward with his head in his hands and sighed, running his hands through his salt and pepper colored hair. "I know it's hard losing a child; no parent should ever have to bury their own before they go," Henry said, "but you know we combed the whole town and campground top to bottom and found nothing."

Ben grabbed a cloth from his pocket and wiped his eyes. "I know," he mumbled, "I just hoped and prayed that something would come up after thirteen years, hell a sticky note or postcard would have sufficed." Ben sighed gravely and wiped his eyes again. "Something happened at that damn campsite. I feel it in my soul."

Henry shrugged his shoulders. "Something could've but don't you think there would've been blood or signs that shit did go down? Maybe she did run off with Donald's boy, even his own dad hasn't heard from him either."

Ben nodded, knowing Henry was probably right. He knew teens do crazy things when they're in love, he hoped that maybe his daughter was different and knew better. "I guess you're right, it's just the thought of her being gone entirely just hurts more than what could've happened."

Henry gave Ben a reassuring pat on the back. "I know bud and I know it hurts talking about her, but I hope one day that you'll be able to find peace." Ben gave Henry a half smile and thanked him. "Don't forget that me and Lilah are just down the road and are here for you."

The friends shook hands and gave each other a parting hug as the auto porch light kicked on and they said their goodbyes. Ben watched Henry get into his car, back out of the driveway and drove off. He cleaned his porch and locked up for the night.

Later, Ben lay in bed asleep when the sound of the screen door opening and slamming shut woke him. He sat up in bed listening for footsteps or motion. Nothing but the sound of cicadas echoed through his house. He quietly climbed out of bed and grabbed his .45 pistol from his nightstand. He made his way out of his room and into the hall, holding his breath to make sure he did not even breathe too loudly. He got down the stairs with ease but once he made it into the living room a foul stench hit his nostrils full force and he gagged.

He cursed under his breath and grabbed a flashlight out of the coat closet. He clicked it and shone the light around the room. As he got closer to the kitchen, the stench grew stronger causing Ben to pull the neckline of his shirt over his nose, in hopes of helping him breathe better. He entered the kitchen and saw the back door off its hinges, covered in scratches and holes. He scanned the room with the light and noticed something hunched over in the corner. It had something red covering it, it was snarling as it was eating.

The coat was torn, some of the inner stuffing poking out

of the rips, stained in a mix of dried mud, blood and mold. The figures' straw colored hair glimmered in the flight as it continued to devour its dinner.

Ben raised his gun up while pulling back the hammer, but then something caught his eye on the jacket: a keychain. He squinted at it and noticed that it was a Tasmanian devil he had bought his daughter for her first day kindergarten. She had always kept with her for luck.

"Tilly," he whimpered. The figure's ears perked up as it turned its head toward Ben. A pale, sunken face with milk-colored eyes and blood smeared around its mouth stared blankly at Ben, tilting its head as if it was studying him.

"Tilly it's me daddy," he whimpered. He placed his gun on the counter and grabbed the Tilly figure. He pulled her close for a hug. He could feel her bones cracking through the jacket. "I'm sorry baby I didn't mean to hurt you," he said, "I've just missed you. I'm sorry I didn't find you sooner. Please forgive me."

Tilly wrapped her arms around Ben, causing them to creak and pop, hugging him. Ben stood there sobbing joyfully until he noticed something. The cicadas, the annoying little buggers that had been chirping nonstop all summer, had suddenly become quiet. Tilly raised her hands away from Ben and stabbed her nails through his back.

He screamed in pain and fell to the floor. Tilly lunged onto him and drove her razor teeth into his neck. His screams became whimpers, then gasps, then silence.

www.ingramcontent.com/pod-product-compliance
Lightning Source LLC
Chambersburg PA
CBHW031130160726
47989CB00017B/2775